I Have a Little Lantern

This book is edited and designed by the Editorial Committee of *Cultural China* series

Story and Illustration by Gan Dayong
Translation by Yijin Wert
Design by Su Liangliang
Copy Editor: Anna Nguyen
Editor: Wu Yuezhou
Editorial Director: Zhang Yicong

Senior Consultants: Sun Yong, Wu Ying, Yang Xinci
Managing Director and Publisher: Wang Youbu

ISBN: 978-1-60220-450-8

Address any comments about *I Have a Little Lantern* to:

Better Link Press
99 Park Ave
New York, NY 10016
USA

or

Shanghai Press and Publishing Development Company, Ltd.
F 7 Donghu Road, Shanghai, China (200031)
Email: comments_betterlinkpress@hotmail.com

Printed in China by Shenzhen Donnelley Printing Co., Ltd.

1   3   5   7   9   10   8   6   4   2

I Have a Little Lantern

我有一盏小灯笼

A Story Told in English and Chinese

By Gan Dayong

Translated by Yijin Wert

Better Link Press

I left for school at dawn. I walked across the quiet fields by myself.

天不亮，我就出发去上学了。我独自穿过寂静的田野。

"I am not scared of anything as long as I have the little lantern with me."

"只要带着小灯笼，我就什么也不怕。"

"Listen! Who is calling my name?"

"听！谁在叫我？"

It was a little spider.

"I feel that there are two monsters behind the wall over there," said the spider.

原来是只小蜘蛛。

小蜘蛛说：“我觉得墙那边有两只怪物。”

"I don't think so. Take my little lantern and you won't be scared. Let's go to school together."

"哪有什么怪物？拿着小灯笼，你就不怕了。我们一起上学去。"

"Hm? Who's there?"

"嗯？那是谁？"

It was a red squirrel.

"I feel like a monster is following me," said the squirrel.

原来是只小松鼠。

小松鼠说："我觉得后面跟着一个怪物！"

"I don't think so. Take my little lantern and you won't be scared. Let's go together through the forest."

"哪有什么怪物？拿着小灯笼，你就不怕了。我们一起来穿过树林。"

"Look! What's that?"

"咦？那是什么啊？"

It was a small hedgehog.

"Shush! I think we are surrounded by monsters," said the hedgehog.

原来是只小刺猬。

小刺猬说："嘘——，小点声，我觉得周围都是妖怪。"

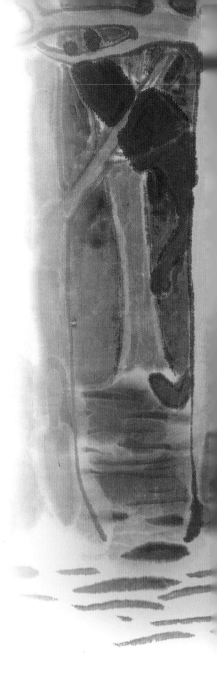

"I don't think so. Take my little lantern and you won't be scared. Let's hurry through."

"哪有什么妖怪? 拿着小灯笼, 你就不怕了。我们快点赶路吧。"

Whoa! It looked like that a giant ball came rolling down the hill.

哇！山坡上滚下一个大圆球。

It was a panda.

"Do you feel it? It could be something terrible. The hill is shaking," said the panda.

原来是一只熊猫。

熊猫说："你们感觉到了么？太可怕了，那座山突然动起来了。"

"I don't think so. Take my little lantern and you won't be scared. We can all go together."

"怎么可能？拿着小灯笼，你就不怕了。来和我们一起走吧。"

"No one should be scared. Even if a monster were to come, this little lantern could drive it away."

"你们都不要怕，就是真的有妖怪来了，小灯笼也会赶跑它。"

But suddenly—

突然——

Just at that moment, a strange-looking monster jumped out in their path.

就在这时，跳出来一个大妖怪，挡住了路。

"Wow wow. I am a giant fierce monster! Give me your little lantern now!" said the monster with a roar.

妖怪大吼道："哇哇哇！我是一个凶狠的大妖怪。快把小灯笼交给我！"

"No, we will never give you the lantern."
We began to fight for the lantern.

"我们才不会把小灯笼给你呢。"
大家抢起了小灯笼。

"You awful monster. You've broken the little lantern."

"讨厌的妖怪，你扯坏了小灯笼。"

"And you're not a monster. You're Xiaohu."

"原来你不是大妖怪。你是小虎。"

Without the light from the lantern, it seemed like monsters surrounded us in the forest.

没有了小灯笼，树林里好像都是妖怪。

Look! There was a little light in the distance.
What was it?

看！远处有个亮亮的小光点。是什么呢？

As the light was moving closer, we realized that it was our teacher.

小光点越来越近，认出来了，原来是老师。

Our teacher came to get us!

是老师来接我们了！

"There is no monster in this world.
Let's go to school together," said the teacher.

老师说：“本来就是没有妖怪的嘛。
现在一起上学去。”

作者的话

In China, children who live in the rural mountain villages need to walk long distance to their schools. Every day, they leave home at dawn and climb over mountains to get to school.

This story is written especially for those who are afraid of walking in the dark. It is a reminder that there is always hope and friendship awaiting them while the journey is lonely and difficult.

在中国，大山里的孩子们要上学，往往要走很远的山路，每天天不亮就要走出家门，翻山越岭去学校。

这故事也献给每一个怕黑、怕走夜路的孩子：路途尽管孤单和艰难，前方依然有希望和温暖。